A Marc Brown **Arthur GOOD SPORTS** Chapter Book

Arthur and the Recess Rookie

Text by Stephen Krensky

Little, Brown and Company

Boston   New York   London

First Edition

The characters and events portrayed in this book are fictitious. Any
similarity to real persons, living or dead, is coincidental and not intended
by the author.

Arthur® is a registered trademark of Marc Brown.

Text has been reviewed and assigned a reading level by Laurel S. Ernst,
M.A., Teachers College, Columbia University, New York, New York;
reading specialist, Chappaqua, New York.

Library of Congress Cataloging-in-Publication Data

Krensky, Stephen.
    Arthur and the recess rookie / text by Stephen Krensky. — 1st ed.
    p. cm. — (A Marc Brown Arthur good sports chapter book)
    Summary: Arthur challenges Francine to a game of kickball to prove to
her that a person does not have to be a great athlete to be important to
the team.
    ISBN 0-316-11916-4 (hc) / ISBN 0-316-12105-3 (pb)
    [1. Teamwork (Sports) — Fiction. 2. Schools — Fiction. 3. Animals —
Fiction.] I. Title.

PZ7.K883 Asm 2001
[Fic] — dc21   00-067857

                    10 9 8 7 6 5 4 3 2 1

                              WOR (hc)
                            COM-MO (pb)

                 Printed in the United States of America

For Tolon Adam Brown

Chapter 1

• • • • • • • • • • •

Rriinnnng!

The bell cut sharply through the air at Lakewood Elementary School. As the ringing stopped, Mr. Ratburn calmly finished up writing a math problem on the blackboard in his third-grade class.

"Take a good look at this problem," he said. "We'll be discussing it when you come back from recess." He paused for a few moments. "All right, you may go."

Everyone hurried out to the playground.

"I hate it when he gives us problems like

that," said the Brain. "It makes it hard to concentrate on recess."

Binky stared at him. "You mean you're actually going to think about it *now?*" He laughed. "WHO WANTS TO PLAY KICK-BALL?"

A crowd of kids gathered quickly.

"I'll be a captain," said Francine.

"I'll be the other," said Binky.

"I'm thinking of a number between one and ten, Binky," said Francine.

Binky scratched his head. "Seven?"

Francine smiled. "Nope. Close, though. So, I get to pick first. Let's see."

She took out a piece of paper and stared at it.

"What's that?" asked Binky.

"Just my list. It reminds me of who's good at what."

"Come on, Francine, hurry up!" said Buster.

Francine frowned. "Don't rush me. These

things take time. There's a lot to keep in mind."

Arthur sighed. "Just keep in mind that recess doesn't last forever."

"All right, all right. I'll take Sue Ellen first."

"Arthur," said Binky.

"Buster."

"Fern."

"Muffy."

They went on picking until only one person was left.

Francine looked around. "I guess that leaves me with George."

George was staring at the ground.

Francine clapped her hands. "Okay, let's take the field. Buster, you're at first. Muffy, go to second. Sue Ellen, take third. Um, George, you're in right field."

George didn't move. His face was still red from having been picked last. In fact,

he wasn't really sure he could claim to have been picked at all. *Last* was just the only thing left after everyone else was taken.

Francine stared at him. "Earth to George — come in, George. You do understand the rules, don't you?"

George nodded.

"Maybe I should explain them again. The pitcher rolls the ball to you at home plate. You kick the ball into the field and run around the bases. If somebody catches your kick in the air, you're out. If somebody throws the ball at you while you're running — and hits you — you're also out. Get it?"

George nodded again.

"Okay. And you know where right field is?"

"Yes. Behind Buster. You know, Francine, I —"

"Great! Then move it!"

As the game started, Francine rolled the

ball to Fern, who was up first. Fern kicked it slowly toward third base and made it to first. The next kicker popped out to Francine, and the third kicked to second for the force-out.

Then Binky was up. He hit the rolling pitch squarely with his toe.

The ball sailed toward right field.

"Come on, George!" yelled Francine. "Get under it!"

George took two steps in, then one back.

"Uh-oh," he muttered.

The ball landed a few feet in front of him and then bounced over his head. By the time he ran it down, Binky was heading for home.

George threw the ball in to Francine. "Sorry," he said.

"You'll get the next one," said Buster.

"That's right," said Muffy.

But Francine said nothing, nothing at all.

Chapter 2

• • • • • • • • • • •

Knock, knock.

"Come in," said Ms. Kroupa, the school nurse. She looked up from her desk to see George standing in the doorway. His face was flushed, and he was shifting his weight from one foot to the other.

"What can I do for you, George?" she asked. "Do you want to sit down?"

"I think so."

She pointed to the couch and motioned for him to sit down.

"Let's see. I know recess just ended, so that explains your red cheeks. Since you came in under your own power and you're not limping, I'm ruling out a broken leg. So far, so good?"

"Yes."

Ms. Kroupa came over for a closer look. "Any new bumps or lumps? Headache or sore throat?"

George shook his head.

"Hmmm. But you have come to see me, after all. There must be something bothering you. Tell me where it hurts."

"Um, well, I'm not sure. The pain moves around."

Ms. Kroupa made a note on a pad. "Moving pain," she repeated. "And where does it move around? On your leg or your arm or where?"

"Yes."

"Yes, what?"

"Um, it hurts in different places at different times."

She made more notes. "Different places at different times. Hmmm. . . . What about

when you play the trumpet? You do play the trumpet, right? Anything then?"

George shook his head. "Oh, no. Nothing to do with the trumpet."

Ms. Kroupa tapped her nose. "Sounds tricky. And when did you start hurting?"

"Well, I noticed it today at recess. I was playing kickball."

"What position?"

"Right field."

Ms. Kroupa nodded. "Ah, yes. I still remember it from my kickball days."

"You do?"

She smiled. "Which tells you something about what a good memory I have. So, was there a particular play when you felt something?"

"No," said George slowly. "It's more of an overall feeling."

Ms. Kroupa scratched her chin. "I see." She scribbled some more. "That could be serious."

"Really?" George tried not to look pleased. "Serious enough to get me out of recess?"

"That *would* be serious," said Ms. Kroupa. "But we don't want to start with such a drastic step. Unless, of course. . . . Is there some reason you want to get out of recess?"

George turned redder. "Why do you say that?"

Ms. Kroupa smiled gently. "I've been a school nurse a long time. But, never mind. . . . Of course, excusing someone from recess requires a number of tests. . . ."

George gulped. "Tests?"

"Certainly. We need to get to the root of the problem. And with the kind of moving pain you describe, it's not always easy."

George started to look uncomfortable. "Would these tests have needles and laser probes?"

"Well," said Ms. Kroupa, "I have to

admit, the laser probes don't come first."

"Don't come first," George repeated. "You know, maybe we should hold off a little. There's no pain now, and maybe it won't come back."

"Maybe," said Ms. Kroupa. "The human body is full of mysteries."

George stood up. "Okay, then. Well, I'll let you know if the pain comes again. I should go back to class now. Thanks. Bye."

"Bye," Ms. Kroupa said, and she watched him go back down the hall.

Chapter 3

• • • • • • • • • • •

"I can't believe it," said Francine, storming into the classroom the next morning.

"Can't believe what?" asked Arthur.

"Ms. Krasny doesn't want me to play the drums in the town parade next week," said Francine. "She doesn't think I'm ready."

"That's too bad," said Arthur. The parade commemorated the founding of Elwood City. He knew how much Francine wanted to be included. "Well, you haven't been playing that long. The others do have more experience."

"I suppose so." Francine frowned. "But

how am I going to get the experience if I don't get the chance to play?"

"I don't know," Arthur admitted. "Was anyone else left out?"

"A few people. But George is getting to march."

"He plays the trumpet, doesn't he?"

Francine nodded. "Luckily, it's a pretty safe instrument."

"What does that mean?"

Francine snorted. "It means he won't get hurt. I can't say the same when he plays kickball."

Arthur looked at her blankly. "You can't?"

"Arthur, haven't you noticed? Yesterday at recess, George could have made an easy catch. And he blew it. The way he lunged for the ball, it might have hit him in the nose."

"Oh, *that* play. Well, he did go to the nurse's office afterward. So maybe he did hurt himself. Anyway, I think George was

14

doing the best he could."

"Well, he needs to do much better if he ever wants me to pick him again for my team."

"Francine, you didn't exactly pick him. He was the only one left."

"Oh. True, but still . . ."

"Picking doesn't always have to be about winning," said Arthur.

Francine laughed. "A lot you know," she said.

"Really, Francine, George hasn't been playing kickball his whole life like the rest of us."

Francine frowned. "They don't have kickball in Sweden?"

"I'm not sure," Arthur admitted. "But even if they do, he might not have that much experience. Besides, why do you always put him in right field?"

Francine snorted. "Because it's the best place to hide him."

"But George isn't going to get any better if he doesn't get a real chance to play."

"Well, that's true." Francine stopped to think. "Oh, I get what you're saying."

"You do?"

"Sure. You want me to work with George."

"Um, Francine . . . ," said Arthur.

"This will be perfect," Francine went on. "George will be putty in my hands. He's ready to be molded . . . to be shaped . . . to be —"

"Francine!"

"What?"

"You don't even know if George is interested."

"Don't be silly, Arthur," Francine said with a smile. "How could he not be interested? Very few people get the chance to be taught by a master."

Chapter 4

After school, Francine went to the gym to practice with the band. George was there, but since he played the trumpet, Francine had never paid him much attention.

"We need to practice," said Ms. Krasny, the music teacher. "The parade, you might say, is just around the corner. So let's begin."

She led them through the first two numbers, stopping at times to correct a wrong note or suggest a change of tempo. Francine was doing her best to keep up, but she was having a hard time. She closed her eyes and sighed.

*   *   *

"We're here at the National Kickball Champ-
ionships, where young Francine Frensky is
putting on quite a show. We've seen great ath-
letes before, and great musicians, too. But
never have we seen one person who was both at
the same time."

Down on the field, Francine was standing
on first base.

"That makes seven hits in a row, doesn't it?"
asked Arthur, the first baseman.

"Eight," Francine corrected him. She ad-
justed her drum across her stomach.

"Sorry," he said. "It's really amazing how
you can run and play the drum at the same
time."

"When you have many abilities," said
Francine, "you can always find new ways to
challenge yourself."

As soon as the next player kicked the ball,
Francine was off like a shot. And as she ran, the
rhythmic tapping of her drum could be heard

across the field. She slid into third base, carefully leaning to one side so she could finish up her drumroll.

"Go, Francine!"
"Keep the beat!"

"Francine?" Ms. Krasny was frowning.
"Um, yes?"

Everyone was staring at Francine.

"I don't know where you were, but I know it wasn't with the rest of us."

"Sorry, Ms. Krasny."

"Francine, you have to keep your mind on the beat. You have to concentrate. If you can't play this standing still, imagine the trouble you'd have if you were marching."

Francine nodded, but she kept her face down.

When the practice was over, Francine headed for the door.

"Don't get discouraged," said a voice behind her.

Francine turned. It was George.

"Discouraged?" Francine forced out a laugh. "I'm not discouraged."

"Well, I know you weren't picked to play in the parade. And then today. . . . Anyway, don't give up."

"Nobody's giving up!" Francine insisted, looking for a way to change the subject. "I was wondering if you wanted to get in some kickball practice. With a little —"

"No, thanks," George said quickly.

"Don't you want to get better?" Francine asked.

"What I want," said George, "is to have a good time."

"Oh," said Francine. And before she could think of anything else to say, George went on his way.

Chapter 5

• • • • • • • • • • •

The next day at lunch, Arthur, Buster, and the Brain were sitting together at their favorite table. Arthur and the Brain were busy eating, but Buster was closely investigating his food.

"Look at this spaghetti," he said. "It's fat!"

"Spaghetti is a form of pasta," said the Brain. "It comes in many thicknesses. There's linguini, fettuccini, angel hair, and —"

"So?" said Buster. "This spaghetti still looks fat to me. It needs to go on a diet. It doesn't really look like spaghetti at all. It looks more like worms. Fat worms."

"That's not actually fair to the worms," said the Brain. "After all, they're just the size they're supposed to be. I don't think they eat junk food or anything."

"Who knows what worms do in secret?" said Buster. "We can't see them under the ground. Maybe they have little junk-food stores. Maybe they stuff their faces with snacks when nobody's looking."

The Brain sighed. "That would be a problem, too, because worms don't have faces."

Buster paused to consider this, and noticed Francine coming in their direction.

"Well, if they did, they might look like that."

He pointed toward Francine, who had been standing behind George in the lunch line. Her expression was far from pleasant.

"What's the matter?" asked Arthur, when she came up to join them.

"He turned me down."

"Who?"

"George."

"Oh," said Arthur. "You mean about helping him with kickball?"

She nodded. "Can you believe that? I mean, it wasn't like I was charging him or anything. And besides, you couldn't put a price on what I would have taught him."

"Well, not everybody loves sports the way you do," said Arthur.

"I know that. But doesn't everybody want to get better? I mean, if you're not getting better, what have you got left?"

"Having fun?" said Arthur.

"That's part of getting better," Francine insisted.

"Well, what if George didn't feel comfortable with you?"

Francine frowned. "Why would he feel like that?"

"Because you always pick him last."

Francine rolled her eyes. "I can't help that. He's the worst player."

"Couldn't you pick him a little sooner once in a while?"

Francine laughed. "That wouldn't exactly help my team's chances of winning."

"Well, winning's not everything."

Francine laughed again.

"What about teamwork?" said Arthur. "I'll bet a team based on cooperation could beat a team based on talent alone."

"Oh, really? Come on, Arthur, be serious."

"I am. I'll give you the first two picks."

"You mean I'll be able to take Binky and Sue Ellen?"

He nodded. "And I'll take George, too."

The Brain cleared his throat. "Excuse me, Arthur, but are you sure this is a good idea? On paper, she will have a distinct advantage."

"Arthur likes a challenge," said Buster.

"That's right," said Arthur. "So, is it a deal?"

Francine shrugged. "Whatever you say. But be prepared — tomorrow will be the worst recess of your life."

Chapter 6

• • • • • • • • • • • •

That night Francine and her family had chicken, mashed potatoes, and peas for dinner. Francine had eaten a little, but mostly she had pushed the chicken and mashed potatoes to one side. That gave her the room to arrange some of the peas in patterns on her plate.

"Someone threw out an antique birdcage today," said Mr. Frensky, who collected trash for the town.

"What are we going to do with *that*, Oliver?" asked Mrs. Frensky.

"Nothing, right away. But I'm going to keep my eye out for an antique bird to go with it." He paused. "Francine?"

"Uh-huh?"

"What are you doing?"

Francine looked up. "Oh. I'm just planning ahead."

"Planning ahead?" said her mother. "With peas?"

"Don't ask," said her sister, Catherine.

"It's my kickball team," Francine explained. "I'm imagining the big game tomorrow at recess."

"What makes this game so big?" asked her father. "Don't you play kickball a lot?"

"Yes, but not like this. You see, Arthur has challenged me. He thinks his team can beat mine."

"Ooooh!" said Catherine. "How exciting. I'll bet all the TV stations will be there."

Francine ignored her. "But that's not the interesting part. He's giving *me* the first two picks."

"Oh?" said her father. "Why would Arthur do that?"

Francine shrugged. "I don't know. Sometimes Arthur gets these crazy ideas. . . . After dinner, I'm going to review all my choices, just to make sure I'm not overlooking anyone."

"Well," said Mr. Frensky, "don't forget to practice your drum."

Francine made a face. "If I don't get to be in the parade, what difference does it make?"

"Now, let's be fair, Francine," said her mother. "Ms. Krasny can't include everyone, and you do have less experience."

"I don't see what you're so worked up about," said Catherine. "It's just a dumb parade."

"Dumb to you, maybe," said Francine. "But not to me."

The parade was just starting down Main

Street. The marchers were trying to keep in step, but they couldn't stay in formation. Like pinballs on the loose, they kept bouncing into one another.

The first float came around the corner. It was shaped like a giant drum, decorated with brass trumpets on the side like frosting on a cake. A single figure stood on the top of the drum waving to the cheering crowd.

It was Francine.

She had her own drum in front of her and held her drumsticks ready. As she looked down at the unruly marchers, she shook her head. Then she began to play.

RAT-A-TAT. RAT-A-TAT. RAT.

As the sound of her drum reached the marchers, they began nodding their heads to the beat. In just a few seconds, they quickly fell into line.

The crowd went wild.

"Francine's saved the day!"

"She's unbeatable!"

"What a girl!"
"Hooray for Francine!"

"Francine, finish your peas," said her mother.

Chapter 7

Francine shook her head. "Your team is doomed, Arthur. D-O-O-M-E-D."

"Thanks for the spelling lesson," he said. "Now, let's play."

They were standing on the playground, having just finished picking the teams for the big game. Francine's team was up first, and Arthur was assigning his players to positions.

"Um, Arthur," said George.

"George, why don't you take second base?" said Arthur.

"Me?" said George. "But I've never played

there. Francine always sticks me in right field."

"Well, I'm not Francine," Arthur answered.

"That's nice of you, Arthur, but I'm not sure —"

"Sssssssh!" said Arthur. "I'm trying to think."

"But —"

"Just go to second base. Please."

George sighed and took his place.

With his players in position, Arthur took a last look around. He felt hopeful. After all, the teams looked evenly matched. The same number of kids were on both sides, and, except for Binky, they were all about the same size.

But from the moment Arthur released the first pitch, things went downhill fast. Francine's team creamed one ball after another. Arthur's players tried to catch them, but they never seemed to reach the ball in time.

For Arthur, the passing minutes seemed like hours. By the time his team finally got up, they were already way behind.

When the bell rang, the score was 17–3.

"I told you so," Francine whispered to Arthur as they returned to class.

Arthur tried to hide his disappointment. This was not the happy ending he had counted on. In all the sports movies he had ever seen, this was the moment where a team like his always won.

But real life wasn't like the movies.

"Arthur?"

"Huh?" Arthur looked up. "Oh, George. Listen, about the game. . . . It wasn't your fault."

"I know that."

"You do?"

"Actually, it was yours."

"Mine?" Arthur gasped.

George nodded. "You made a mistake, Arthur."

"I did?"

George nodded again. "Well, a few, really. I mean, you were right that Francine's team could be beaten."

"I was? But then . . . what was the mistake?"

"Trying to play as though both teams were the same."

Arthur looked confused. "Well, what else could we do?"

"This," said George, whispering his plan into Arthur's ear.

Francine was just sitting down at her desk when Arthur marched up to her.

"We want a rematch," he declared.

Francine was shocked. "A what?"

"You heard me," Arthur said. "We want to play you again."

"But, Arthur, it was *sooooo* painful out there. Why would you want to go through that again?"

"I admit we got off to a slow start. Next time will be different."

Francine shook her head. "It wouldn't be fair, Arthur."

Arthur sniffed at the air. "Smells like chicken to me. . . ."

"CHICKEN?" Francine's mouth dropped open. "Nobody's chicken! If being pulverized is what you want, then being pulverized is what you'll get. But there'll be no mercy, get it? None at all."

Arthur smiled. "We wouldn't want it any other way."

Chapter 8

• • • • • • • • • • •

By the next morning, news of the rematch had traveled around the school. Had Arthur gone crazy? Would Francine show mercy? Quite a few kids skipped their own games to stand on the sidelines and watch.

Francine was feeling very confident as she approached the plate. Her team had destroyed Arthur's the day before. And she was ready to do it again.

Already Muffy was on first and Sue Ellen on second. All she had to do was drive them in.

As Arthur got ready to pitch, George

called for a time-out. He ran in from right field for a private talk.

"Is it time?" asked Arthur.

George nodded. "Francine only kicks to left field. If we shift the outfielders over, we can cover more ground."

"But if we leave right field open, won't she just hit it there?"

George smiled. "Maybe. But when you try something that isn't natural, you make mistakes. Besides," he added, "what have we got to lose?"

Arthur couldn't argue with that. He turned to his outfielders and motioned them over.

"Hey!" Francine called out from the plate. "What's going on?"

"Just a little strategy," said Arthur.

Francine frowned. The four outfielders were all standing to the left of second base.

"Can they do that?" she asked.

"Player placement is not specified in any rule," said the Brain.

"But right field's wide open," hissed Binky. "Just hit it there!"

Francine nodded. As Arthur rolled the ball toward her, she swung her foot awkwardly, popping the ball up for Fern to catch at first base.

"One out!" cried Arthur.

Binky was up next. But again, before Arthur started his windup, George called for a time-out.

"Another shift?" asked Arthur.

George shook his head. "Not with Binky. He hits to all fields. But he does get impatient waiting for the ball. If you pitch to him *really* slowly, I think it will help."

"Okay," said Arthur.

George retook his position, and Arthur turned to the plate.

"Come on, already," said Binky. "We haven't got all day."

Arthur nodded. He swung his arm back, but when he released the ball, he let it fall off his fingers.

The ball rolled and rolled and rolled. Binky's head traced a circle over and over again following the ball's movement. By the time the ball actually reached him, he was feeling a bit dizzy.

He wound up for a big kick, swung hard at the ball — and missed.

"Strike one!" said Arthur.

"No more tricks," said Binky, as the ball was thrown back to Arthur.

Arthur just shrugged. Then he threw the ball slowly again.

This time Binky connected. But he was so nervous about missing that he toed the ball right up the middle.

Arthur caught it — and Binky was out.

After that, the rest of Francine's team fell apart. The third out came quickly, and

when Arthur's team came up, they pounded the ball for five runs.

At the end of recess, Arthur's team was ahead, 8–2. As the teammates congratulated one another, Arthur thanked George for speaking up.

"How did you figure all that stuff out?" he asked.

George smiled. "Well," he said, "I've had a lot of free time in right field. I guess I finally put it to good use."

Chapter 9

• • • • • • • • • • • •

Francine's face was a mixture of shock and frustration as she returned to the classroom. Both Muffy and Sue Ellen were patting her on the back, trying to make her feel better.

"I can't believe we lost," Francine said, slumping down into her seat. "We had better players. Much better."

"Don't worry," said Sue Ellen. "I'm sure the pain will go away someday."

"Well, it wasn't like everyone was watching," Muffy said. "I saw three girls playing jump rope in the corner."

Francine stared into space. "It should have been simple," she went on. "I don't get it. . . ."

"They outwitted us," said the Brain.

Francine frowned. "What do you mean?"

"Arthur's team didn't try to outhit us or outthrow us," the Brain explained. "They used strategy."

"Strategy!" Francine snorted. "That's not fair! Whoever heard of strategy in kickball?"

The Brain shrugged. "I guess Arthur has. You can ask him yourself. Here he comes."

Arthur was trying to keep from smiling too widely, but he was having a hard time of it.

"Kind of gloomy over here," he said.

"Yeah, yeah," said Francine. "Just gloat and get it over with."

"Gloat? Me?" Arthur clutched at his chest.

"All right, all right," Francine muttered. "Maybe you were right. There is more to kickball than I thought."

"Actually," said Arthur, "there's more to kickball than *I* thought, too. I can't take the credit for all those shifts and special plays. George thought of most of them."

"George?" sputtered Francine. "George, who can barely catch the ball or kick it in a straight line? *That* George? What does he know about kickball?"

The Brain shrugged. "Apparently more than we do."

Francine didn't have a chance to talk with George until their band practice after school. Francine was warming up with a marching drumroll when George joined in with matching toots on his trumpet.

They played together for a minute before Francine stopped for a break. "That sounded pretty good," she said.

"We play together pretty well," said George.

"Better than this morning, anyway," said Francine. "That was quite a game you pulled off today," she said.

George blushed. "Well, we got lucky, catching you by surprise and all."

"I thought you were a recess rookie," said Francine. "Boy, was I wrong."

"Thanks," said George.

"Yup, I've learned my lesson. It's too bad there aren't any kickball strategies to use against Arthur."

"Oh, there are," said George. "You just have to know where to look."

"Really?" said Francine. "How interesting."

George hesitated. "You know, Francine, strategies can work for all kinds of things — not just sports."

"What do you mean?"

"Well, I know how you want to be in the parade."

She sighed. "It might seem silly to some people, but I hate feeling like I don't really matter."

"I know what you mean," said George. "It's kind of like always being stuck in right field."

"Okay, okay," said Francine. "But at least you got to be in the game. I just wish there was a way I could march and do *something* in the parade."

George smiled. "Actually," he said, "there is."

Chapter 10

• • • • • • • • • • •

The Elwood City Founders' Parade was into its second block when they saw her.

"Hey, Francine!" yelled Arthur.

"Over here!" added Buster.

"Say 'Cheese'!" shouted Muffy, clicking her camera.

Francine was on the right side of the marching band. They were dressed in matching uniforms, although Francine had extra gold braiding on her sleeves.

"Francine must be a general or admiral or something," said Binky.

"I don't believe this band has ranks," said the Brain.

"Well, I'm going to salute anyway," said Binky. "Just to be safe."

Francine was glad to see her friends in the crowd. She couldn't wave back, though, because her hands were busy holding a pole. At the other end of it was an American flag. It fluttered in the breeze.

George was marching a few steps behind her. He couldn't even smile because his mouth was busy with his trumpet, but he tilted it toward Arthur and the others.

As Francine passed in front of Arthur, he gave her a look.

"So, Francine, who are you going to pick first at recess tomorrow?" Arthur asked.

She smiled again at all of them, but then turned back to look at George. "You'll just have to wait and see," she said, and raised the flag just a little higher as she continued marching down the street.